...ate of Membership

This is to certify that

_____

is an honorary member of the

LITERARY CRITTERS GUILD

as of the date

_____

William ShakesBEAR

Signed William Shakesbear, spokesbear
of the Literary Critters Guild

Good day, dear friend!

Allow me to be the first to congratulate you on becoming the newest member of the wonderful Literary Critters Guild! I am thrilled you share a love of all things reading, writing, and books. I look forward to sharing ideas with you and reading your future literary works.

Speaking of ideas, alas, I write to you in a state of UN-spiration. This will surely be the winter of my discontent if I don't find an idea to write my next play about. I should be hibernating but will not even think of sleeping without first finding my inspiration. To have no ideas to write about is simply too much to BEAR (pun intended).

I've decided to go off and gather inspiration from some of my talented Literary Critter friends. Wish me luck! The future of theater depends on it!

Your very inspiration-less friend,

William ShakesBEAR

"Boldness be my friend!" William declared as he bounded out of his cave, off on his journey for inspiration.

As William walked through the woods, he came upon
Mole Dahl, who popped up from a hole in the ground.
"Dear Mole, I'm in search of some inspiration.
What do you think I should write about?"

"Will, use your imagination—
it could be anything at all ...

A cunning fox! A chocolate bar! A newt in a drinking glass—anything!
Just make it OUTRAGEOUSLY fantastical. A little magic can take you
a long way!"

William thought Mole's ideas were wonderful, but a little too wild for
his play. So, bidding him farewell, William set off to find someone with
a good storytelling sense and sensibility ...

Walking down the path, William spotted Crane Austen.

"Dear Crane! Do you have an idea for my play? My mind is a blank ..."

"Don't overthink it, Will. The best stories are based on relationships. Why not write about painting in the countryside with your friend?" And with that she handed her paintbrush to William.

"How lovely! I fear it might be TOO simple though."

Just then, a rabbit jumped up from the flowers and hopped away. William recognized the animal, so he said farewell to Crane and ran off to catch it.

Crane called after him, "If a story is well-written, I always find it too short. Good luck!"

William managed to wrangle the rabbit, who was named Peter. He belonged to Beatrix Trotter, who was delighted to see them. "Peter! THERE you are. My thanks to you, Will!"

"Not at all, Mrs. Trotter!" said William, placing Peter down next to his sibling Benjamin. "Can you help a bear out? I need literary inspiration …"

"Get yourself a pet, William!" said Beatrix. "My bunnies get up to such mischief, I can't help but write about their antics."

"Thank you," said William, "but a pet is too much responsibility for me. When I'm not writing, I sleep for MONTHS on end!"

"I wish you the best of luck," said Beatrix, plucking a carrot from her garden. "There is something delicious about writing the first words of a story. You never know where they'll take you."

William thanked Beatrix and went on his way.

Soon the path he was on became an open road. Will saw Yak Kerouac, walking quickly and carrying a suitcase.

"Ah, Yak! Just the fellow, I—"

"No time to talk, Will! I'm on my way to EVERYWHERE!"

"But I need to find some inspiration for my new play. Can you help?"

"I have nothing to offer anybody except my own confusion! Besides, the best teacher is experience."
And with that, Yak Kerouac ran off down the road.

William shrugged, closed his eyes, and let his feet take him where they wanted to go.

His feet led him to
Edgar Talon Crow's treehouse.

William could have just called up to him,
but there was a door drawn on the tree's
trunk, so he politely knocked on it.

"Who's that tapping at my treehouse
door?" cawed Edgar.

"It's William Shakesbear, good Crow!
Can you help me find some inspiration
for my play?"

KNOCK HERE PLEASE

Edgar invited him up.

While looking for a smaller tree, William noticed some shuffling and snuffling in the grass.

"C. S. Shrewis!" said William. "Just the literary shrew I wanted to see.

Can you help me find inspiration for my story?"

C. S. poked up his snout and twitched his whiskers.
"Just follow a path and go with it! You might find mythological creatures, kings and queens, maybe even a tasty box of Turkish delight—inspiration is everywhere!"

Before William could thank him, Shrewis disappeared into a tiny wooden wardrobe.

"I don't think he's coming back," said Loris Carroll, passing William a cup of tea.

"You startled me, Loris! Did you see what just happened?! Shrewis DISAPPEARED into that wardrobe! IMPOSSIBLE!"

Loris blinked slowly. "Why, sometimes I've believed as many as six impossible things before breakfast. It's magical nonsense like this that should inspire your play!

That, and the mad tea party we're about to have."

"A tea party?"

William was delighted to join the curious affair that included more Literary Critter friends.

"What the dickens, even Charles Chickens is here!"

"Please, sir, may I have some more?" clucked Charles.

"This is just delightful!" said William, but he thought
it was a bit too silly for him to write about.

Full of tea and cake, William visited Wagatha Christie next.

"Greetings, Wagatha!" said William. "Can you help me decide what to write my play about? I have no clue …"

"Clues are hard to find," said Wagatha, chewing on a bone. "Why not write about being a supersleuth, sniffing out clues to solve a mystery!"

"Ooh, how thrilling!" said William.

Wagatha continued, "Remember, very few of us are what we seem. Take this innocent-looking squirrel for example. I have evidence to suggest he's been burying acorns in MY garden!"

"Well, you're always barking up MY tree!" squeaked the squirrel.

"Crime doesn't pay!!" Wagatha barked back.

As William watched Wagatha chase the squirrel up a tree, he decided that might be his clue to exit.

William was growing tired as he wandered down to the stream.
There he saw Langston Mews, stretched out at his typewriter.

"Good day, Langston! Can you help inspire my writing?" asked William.

"Why not write a poem?" Langston pointed to the stream. "Listen to the flowing water—it sounds like music if you pay attention. Poetry could flow from you like jazz!"

William thought that was a
marvelous idea, but as they sat and
listened to the water flow, William began
to get sleepy. He decided it was time to say
goodbye and head home.

Langston called out to him,
"Hold fast to your dreams,
Will! I know you'll write
a wonderful play!"

My soul has
grown deep
like a river

On his way home, William muttered to himself, "It's been a grand day, but I'm still not sure what to write about."

Just then, little Chicktor Hugo fluttered onto his shoulder. He chirped, "You have flowers at your feet and stars above you ... what better inspiration could you ask for?"

William nodded. "It's a beautiful evening, but I'm too sleepy now to create."

"Remember, nothing is more powerful than an idea whose time has come. And you'll have an idea soon enough, Will. Sweet dreams!"

Chicktor Hugo skipped away into the night, and William Shakesbear returned to his cave to do what tired-out bears like him do in winter —hibernate.

"Perchance to dream, and all that …"

CAVE OF WILLIAM SHAKESBEAR

And William DID, in fact, dream. He dreamt of hidden acorns and tiny wardrobes, cups of tea and lovely cakes, of funny bunnies and cute newts, of star-studded skies, tree climbing, winding rivers, and endless roads.

His dreams were deep and sweet, and he slept all winter through.

When springtime arrived, after a long winter of dream-filled slumber, a well-rested William awoke and emerged from his cave. There he discovered a pile of BRAND-NEW BOOKS gifted to him by his friends. He rejoiced in the thought of the inspiration he might find between their pages.

CAVE OF WILLIAM SHAKESBEAR

YAK KEROUAC

MOLE DAHL

OSCAR WILD

Finally, William was ready to write his play.

Glad tidings, dear friend!

I write to you with joy in my heart as I have FOUND my inspiration!

Alas, I have again slept through winter but I am now rested and ready to pen my play! It will be titled "A Winter-Long Dream," and it shall be an ode to the wonderful members of the Literary Critters Guild - my friends who I am so fortunate to know! Maybe it will help to attract more members and spread our love of reading and storytelling far and wide!

My dear friend, as you have recently become a fully-fledged Guild member, I simply must ask, what will YOU be reading or writing about next?

Your friend and proud Literary Critters spokesbear,

William ShakesBEAR 🐾

Special thanks to...

ROALD DAHL

MAYA ANGELOU

JANE AUSTEN

AGATHA CHRISTIE

BEATRIX POTTER

LEWIS CARROLL

EDGAR ALLEN POE

C.S. LEWIS

JACK KEROUAC

WILLIAM SHAKESPEARE

GEORGE ORWELL

THE BRONTË SISTERS

OSCAR WILDE

LANGSTON HUGHES

T.S. ELIOT

VICTOR HUGO

WILLIAM WORDSWORTH

CHARLES DICKENS

ZONDERKIDZ

Literary Critters
Copyright © 2022 by Sophie Corrigan
Illustrations © 2022 by Sophie Corrigan

Requests for information should be addressed to:
Zonderkidz, 3900 *Sparks Dr. SE, Grand Rapids, Michigan 49546*

Library of Congress Cataloging-in-Publication Data

LCCN 2021054635 (print) | LCCN 2021054636 (ebook) | ISBN
9780310734093 (hardcover) | ISBN 9780310734109 (ebook)
LC record available at https://lccn.loc.gov/2021054635
LC ebook record available at https://lccn.loc.gov/2021054636

Zonderkidz is a trademark of Zondervan

Design: Diane Mielke

Printed in South Korea

22 23 24 25 26 27 /SAM/ 13 12 11 10 9 8 7 6 5 4 3 2 1